I WANT TO DRAW CARS

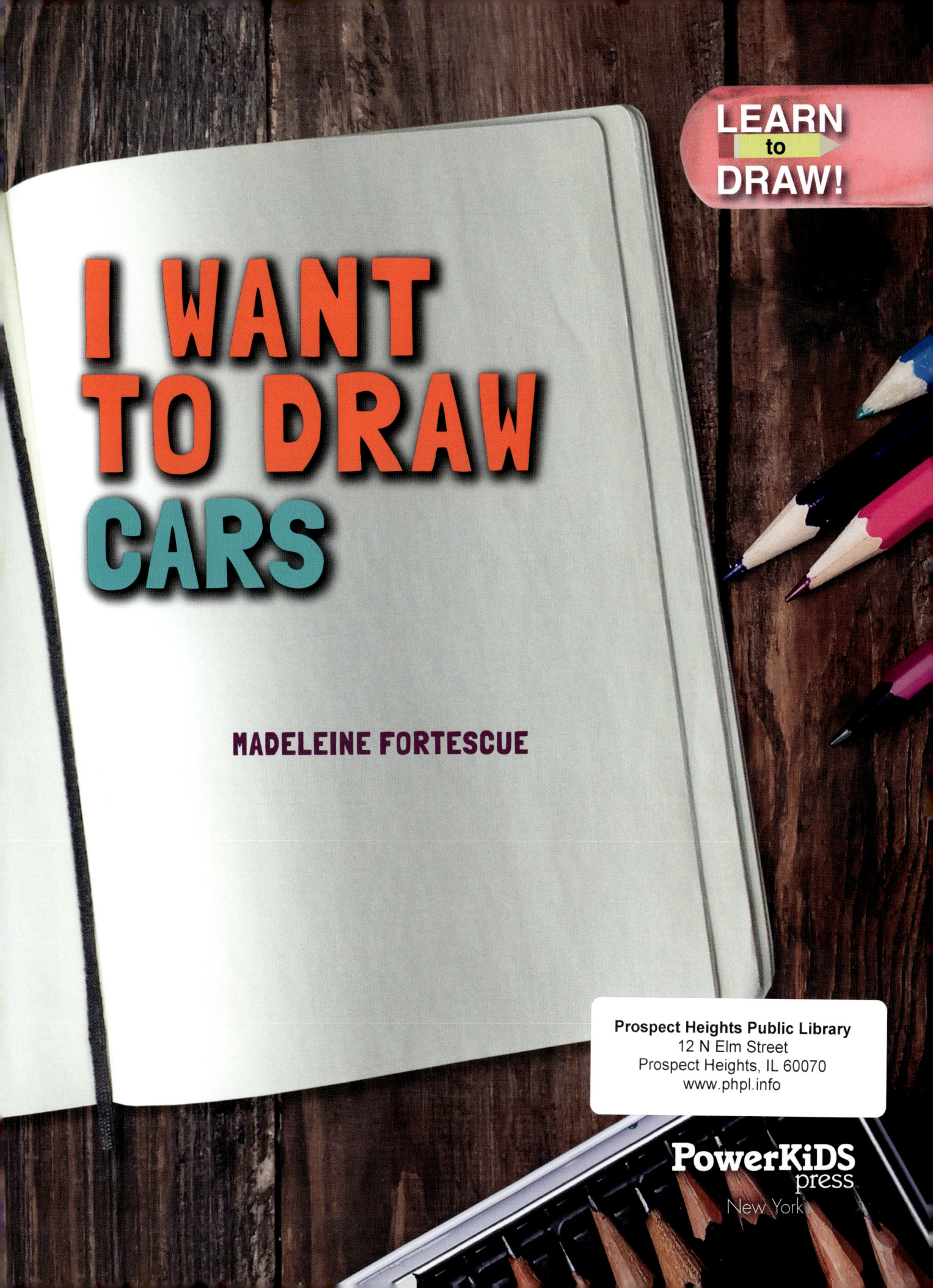

MADELEINE FORTESCUE

PowerKids press
New York

Published in 2019 by The Rosen Publishing Group, Inc.
29 East 21st Street, New York, NY 10010

Copyright © 2019 by The Rosen Publishing Group, Inc.

All rights reserved. No part of this book may be reproduced in any form without permission in writing from the publisher, except by a reviewer.

Copyright 2001; reprint 2019

Editor: Greg Roza
Book Design: Tanya Dellaccio

Photo Credits: Front Cover, back cover, pp. 1, 3–24 Chiociolla/Shutterstock.com; cover Ariadna22822/Shutterstock.com; p. 5 (pencil and sharpener) KET-SMM/Shutterstock.com; p. 5 (girl) Rusian Guzov/Shutterstock/com; p. 6 Science & Society Picture Library/SSPL/Getty Images; p. 8 Three Lions/Hulton Archive/Getty Images; p. 10 Heritage Images/Hulton Archive/Getty Images; p. 12 happymay/Shutterstock.com; p. 14 Mauvries/Shutterstock.com; p. 16 RacingOne/ISC Archives/Getty Images; p. 18 Gustavo Fadel/Shutterstock.coml; p. 20 Lissandra Melo/Shutterstock.com.

Cataloging-in-Publication Data

Names: Fortescue, Madeleine.
Title: I want to draw cars / Madeleine Fortescue.
Description: New York : PowerKids Press, 2019. | Series: Learn to draw! | Includes glossary and index.
Identifiers: LCCN ISBN 9781508167761 (pbk.) | ISBN 9781508167747 (library bound) | ISBN 9781508167778 (6 pack)
Subjects: LCSH: Automobiles in art–Juvenile literature. | Drawing–Technique–Juvenile literature.
Classification: LCC NC825.A8 F67 2019 | DDC 743'.89629222-dc23

Manufactured in the United States of America

CPSIA Compliance Information: Batch CS18PK: For Further Information contact Rosen Publishing, New York, New York at 1-800-237-9932

CONTENTS

Drawing Cars 4
Drawing the Benz ....
    Three-Wheeler............. 6
Drawing the Ford Model T 8
Drawing the Bugatti
    41 Royale 10
Drawing the Volkswagen
    Beetle 12
Drawing the Chevrolet Bel Air
    Sport Coupe 14
Drawing the Shelby
    AC Cobra 16
Drawing the McLaren F1 18
Drawing the Plymouth
    Prowler 20
Drawing Terms 22
Glossary 23
Index 24
Websites 24

DRAWING CARS

Have you ever sat in a car and wondered how it works? Have you ever wanted to drive a car to see how fast it goes? Well, you're not old enough to drive yet, but you are old enough to think about your dream car.

There are many different kinds of cars. Cars have basic parts, such as tires, engines, bumpers, and fenders. Each car has an individual style and look that tells us something about when it was made. In this book, you will learn about eight cars, from an 1885 three-wheeler to a 1990s **hot rod**! You will also learn about the creators of these cars.

The first car you will draw—the Benz Three-Wheeler— looks a little funny with only three wheels, but that's how it was built. There are directions under each drawing to help you through each step. Each new step of your drawing is shown in color to help guide you.

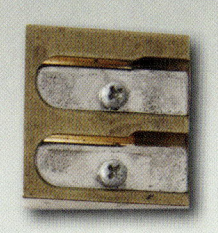

Ready to draw? Make sure you have a pencil, pencil sharpener, an eraser, and a sketchbook.

DRAWING THE BENZ THREE-WHEELER

German **engineer** Karl Benz made the first motorcar in 1885. Unlike the cars of today, this car had only three wheels, with two wheels in the back and one wheel in the front. Its engine was called a two-stroke engine, which made it go at a speed of only eight miles (12.9 km) per hour. That speed is slow when you think about today's cars. Today's cars can go as fast as 276 miles (444 km) per hour!

Although the Benz Three-Wheeler was built more than 100 years ago, it had some parts that are still used in the cars of today. These parts include a water-cooled engine, an electric **ignition**, and a **differential gear**.

The first Benz automobile was sometimes called the Benz Tricycle.

1

Draw three circles. The first circle is larger than the one that crosses it. Add the third circle, which is the smallest, as shown here.

2

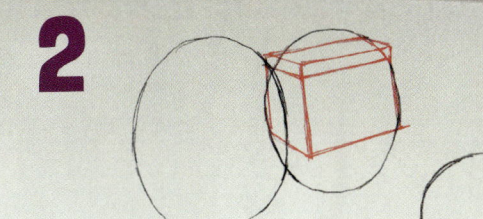

Next, draw a rectangle inside the circle in the middle. Draw a second rectangle a little higher and to the left of the first one. Draw two lines at both ends of the rectangles to join them. Next, add lines to the top of the box to make a lid.

3

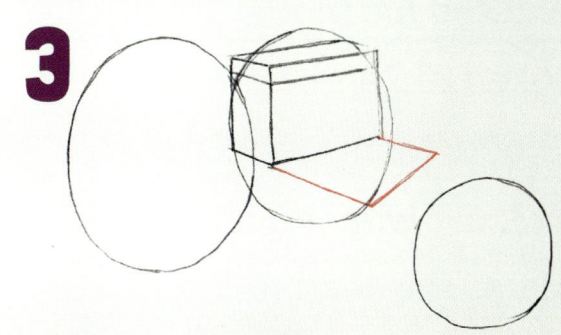

Add a funny-shaped rectangle. Notice how each side of this rectangle is a different size. Connect this rectangle to the bottom of the box you just drew.

4

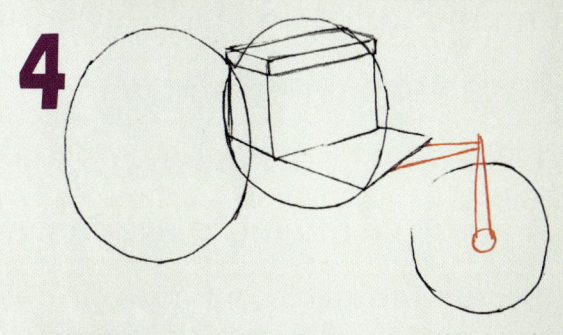

Next, draw two lines that come to a point away from the funny-shaped rectangle. Now draw two more lines that continue from the first lines. This set of lines should also come to a point. Notice how the two sets of lines meet at the points. Draw a tiny circle within the smallest circle.

5

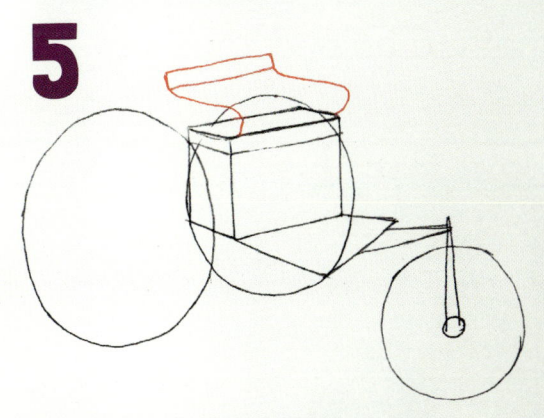

Draw two curved lines on top of the lid of the box. Join them by adding a small rectangle at the top of the curved lines.

6

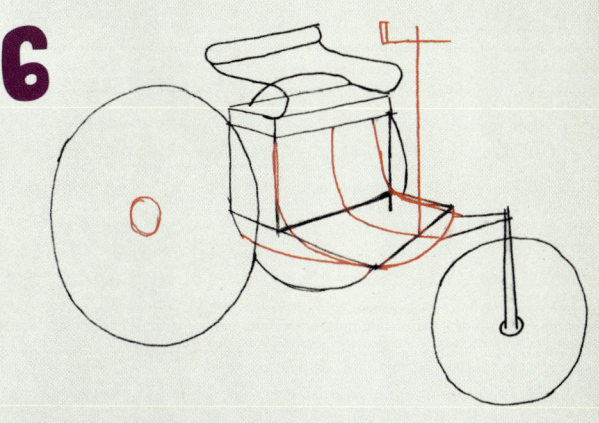

Curve the lines of the funny-shaped rectangle and the bottom of the box. Add a small circle to the biggest circle. Then add a vertical line starting at the bottom of the funny-shaped rectangle. Add a horizontal crossing the vertical line. Then add the small handle at the left end of the horizontal line.

7

DRAWING THE FORD MODEL T

Henry Ford made the Model T in Detroit, Michigan, in 1908. In a 1922 race, Noel Bullock entered his Model T car, which he named "Old Liz." The car looked old and worn down, since it was unpainted and without a hood. Many people said it looked like a tin can. However, Bullock's car won the race, even against some of the more expensive cars. This lead to the Model T being nicknamed "Tin Lizzie."

With the Model T car, Henry Ford changed the way cars were built. He began the first **assembly-line** production of a car. In an assembly line, each worker does one job toward making each individual product. This method helped keep the cost of the Model T low.

The Ford Model T was a very popular car. It was easy to drive and keep in good shape.

1

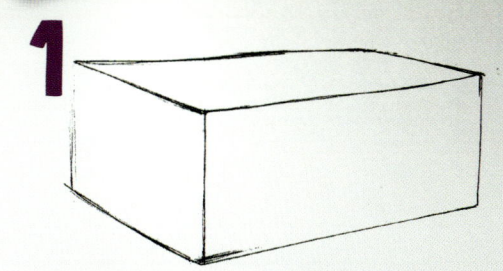

Begin by drawing a 3-D box to guide your drawing.

2

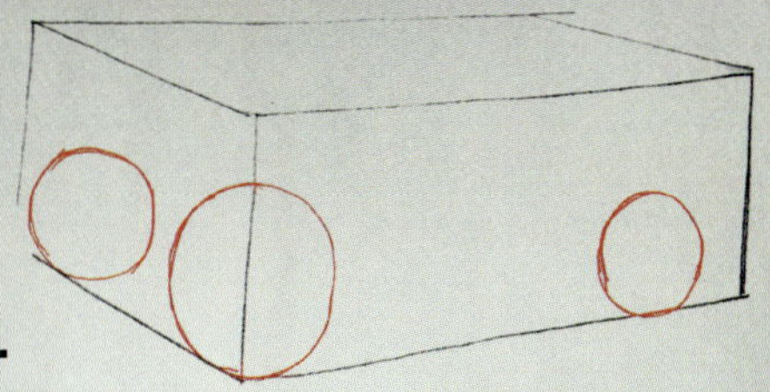

Now draw three circles inside the box. Notice the three sizes and where the circles are placed.

3

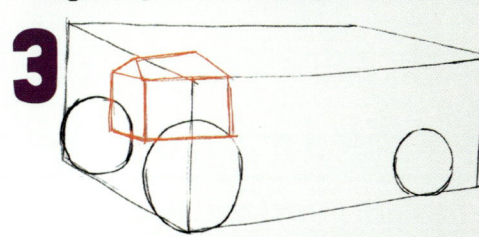

Next, draw a shape like a house at the front end of the box. This will be the front end and engine.

4

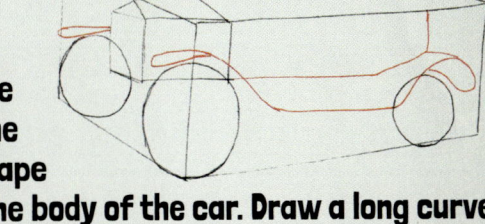

Extend the lines of the house-shape to form the body of the car. Draw a long curved line to make the fender. Draw two shapes like a paddle above the two circles (wheels) at the left to make the tops of the fenders.

5

Now draw the front window by making a slanted rectangle. Then draw the front and back seats by making two sets of curved lines behind the window.

6

Draw in the details of the car. First, draw the steering wheel and the car horn. Draw in the two car doors by making two "U" shapes on the side of the car as shown.

7

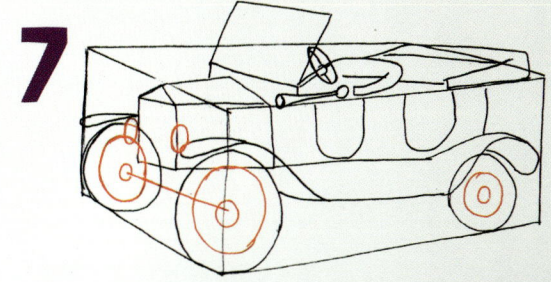

Draw two smaller circles within each of the larger circles at the front of the car. Connect the two smallest circles in the front wheels with a straight line. Next, add two small oval shapes at the front of the car for the headlights. These ovals should touch the paddle-shaped tops of the fenders.

8

Next, add seven or eight vertical lines to the front grille. Then add small curved lines to the seats. Add two slanted lines to the top of the back seat to make the hood. Finish your drawing by erasing any extra lines.

9

DRAWING THE BUGATTI 41 ROYALE

Ettore Bugatti was the designer of the Bugatti 41 Royale. As a teenager, Ettore studied art. However, he decided not to become an artist because he became interested in making and racing motorcars. In 1898, he built his first car. Ettore began his own car company in 1910. He soon began to win races and became recognized for his race cars.

Stories say a British lady told Ettore that although he was known for making the fastest cars, Rolls-Royce was known for making the best cars. This comment pushed Ettore to build a luxury car. The Bugatti 41 Royale was the most powerful and elegant car made at that time. This model of car was built from 1929 to 1932.

The design of the Royale was based on horse-drawn carriages. These cars were meant to be driven by a chauffeur, who is a person hired to drive a car.

1 First, draw a 3-D box to guide your drawing.

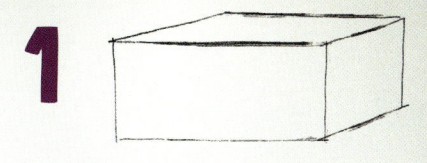

2 To the left of the box, draw a wider and taller box touching the first one.

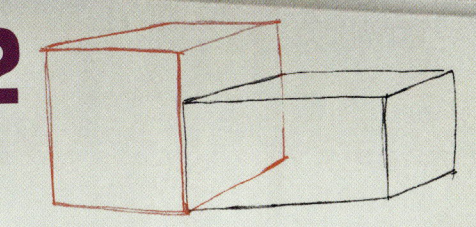

3 Draw three circles for the wheels. The largest circle touches the shortest box. Draw the second circle away from the largest circle and the box. Add the third circle at the bottom and to the left of the tallest box.

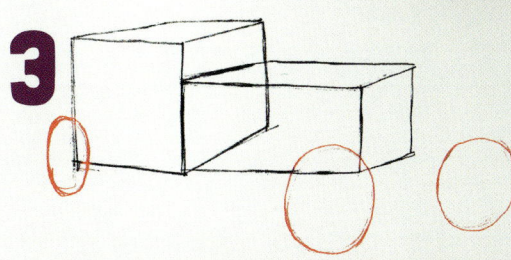

4 Next, draw long curved lines to make the fender. Then add a shape that looks like a large kidney bean to the circle at the far right. This will be the fender on the other side of the car.

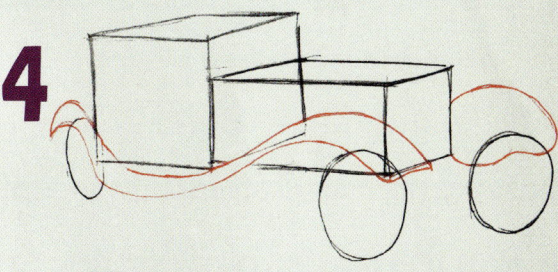

5 Now make the top corners in both of the boxes rounded, or curved. There are eight corners in all. Next, add a curved line on the side of the shorter box.

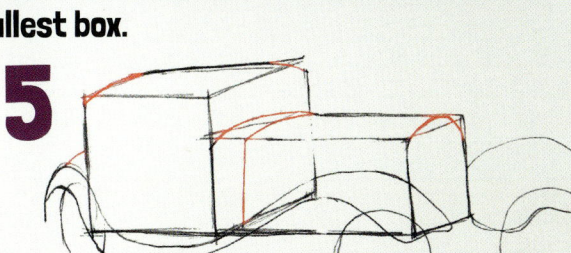

6 Add a rectangle to the top of the side of the tallest box. Notice how this rectangle slants. Draw the second rectangle on the side of the tallest box, but near the top. Notice how this rectangle has rounded corners. Add the third rectangle below the second, rounded one.

7 Draw six more circles at the right of the shortest box, which make the car's headlights and horns. Now, draw a long, thin rectangle that touches the two circles of the wheels at the right. This shape, which is the bumper, is placed at the front of the car.

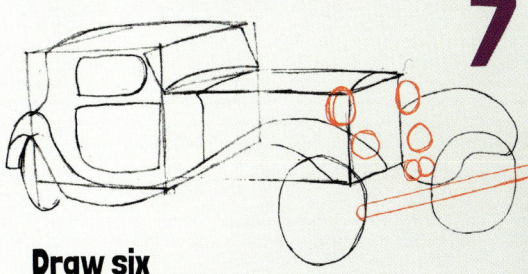

8 Draw circles within each of the three circles, making the car's wheels. Add vertical lines to make the car's grille. Draw a small rectangle on top of the bumper to make the **license plate**. Add one more curved line along the fender, below the rectangle that is the car door. Finish your drawing by erasing any extra lines.

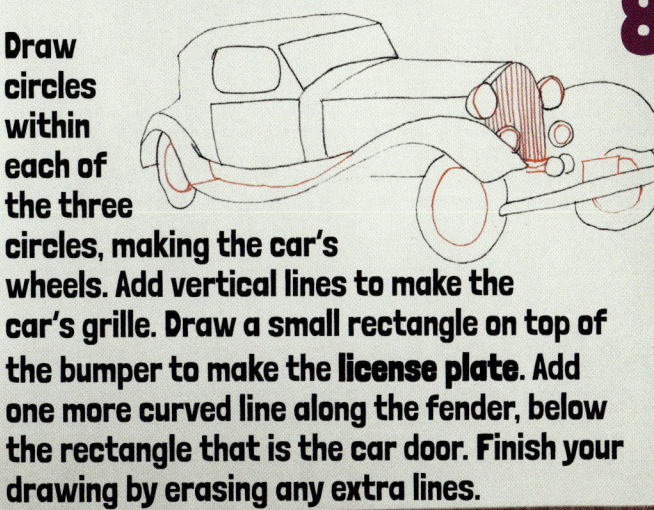

DRAWING THE VOLKSWAGEN BEETLE

The Volkswagen was a popular car in the 1960s. The model was nicknamed the "Beetle" because of its bug-like shape. Austrian engineer and car designer Ferdinand Porsche and Adolf Hitler—who was the leader of Germany from 1933 to 1945—were eager to make a car that all German people could afford. The Volkswagen, which in German means "people's car," began production during World War II (1939–45).

Soon after the war ended, the Volkswagen Beetle was brought to the United States from Germany. It was not very popular in the beginning because of its link with Hitler. But the car's low price soon made the Beetle a huge sensation. In 1998, a new version of the Beetle hit the market.

The Volkswagen Beetle was also nicknamed "the Bug." The 1969 movie *The Love Bug* featured the popular car as a character named Herbie.

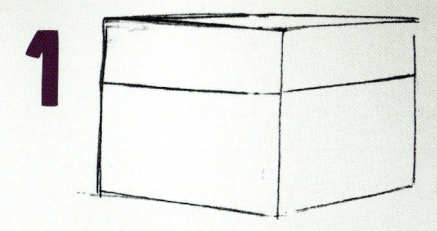

1 Draw two 3-D boxes, one stacked on top of the other. This should look like a box with a lid.

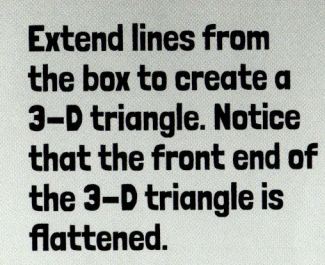

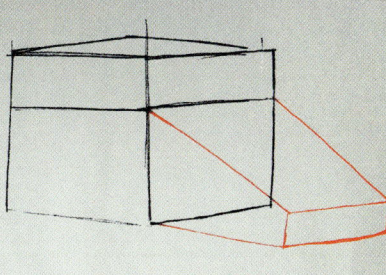

2 Extend lines from the box to create a 3-D triangle. Notice that the front end of the 3-D triangle is flattened.

3 Next, draw three circles for the wheels. Notice that the circle farthest right is smaller than the other two circles.

4 Now round out the corners of the top of the box by curving the lines at the corners. Next, curve the lines on the tops and sides of the triangular shape.

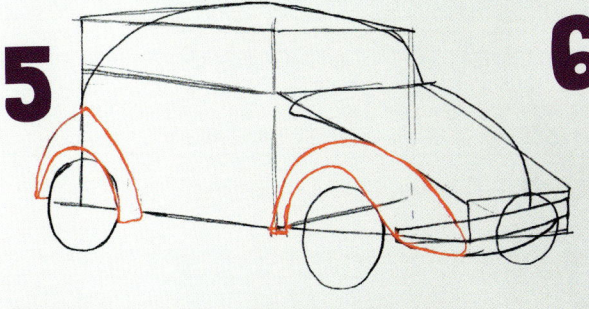

5 Next, draw curved lines halfway around the two largest wheels. These are the fenders of the Beetle.

6 Draw three rectangles in the lid of the box. Notice how each is a different size. Also, draw each rectangle with curved ends. These rectangles are the windows of the Beetle.

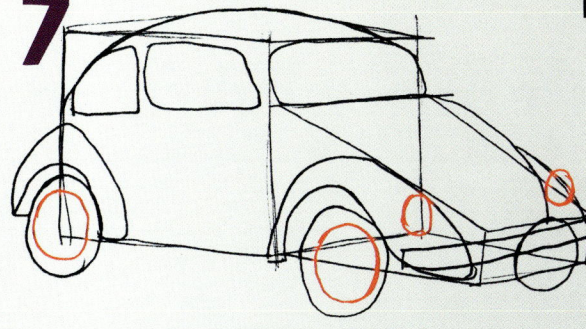

7 Next, add two more circles to the front of the car to make the headlights. Then draw two smaller circles inside the larger circles that form the wheels.

8 Draw a rectangle to make the car door. Draw a vertical line in the window to form a smaller window. Clean up your drawing by erasing any extra lines.

13

DRAWING THE CHEVROLET BEL AIR SPORT COUPE

In 1911, Louis Chevrolet and William C. Durant started an automobile division of General Motors that is now known as Chevrolet, or Chevy. In 1955, Chevrolet made the legendary Bel Air Sport Coupe. What made the Bel Air so special was its **V8 engine**, which helped the car reach 93 miles (149 km) per hour. The V8 engine had a few nicknames, such as "Turbo-Fire" and the "Hot One."

In the first year it was built, the Bel Air won many car races, including one for the National Association for Stock Car Automobile Racing (NASCAR). The Bel Air did so well as a racing car that it was chosen to be the official **pace car** for the world-famous Indianapolis 500.

The sporty Bel Air was produced in hardtop and convertible models.

1 Draw a long 3-D box.

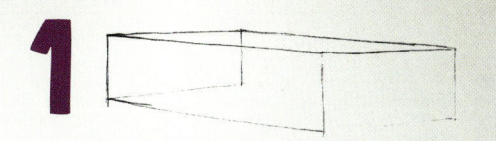

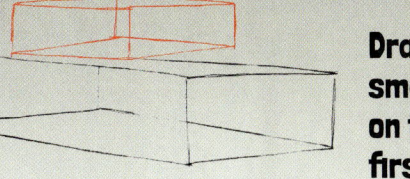

2 Draw a smaller box on top of the first one.

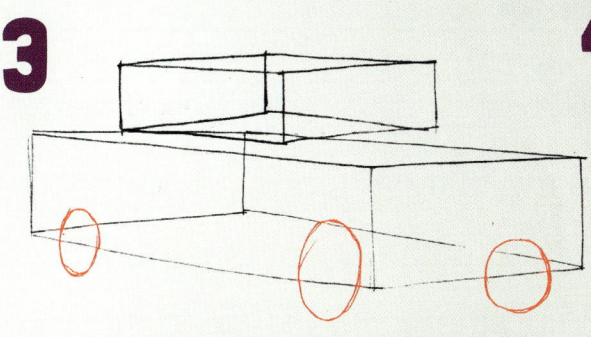

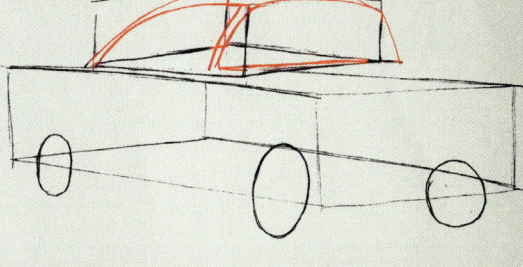

3 Draw three circles to make the wheels. Notice their different sizes and where they are placed in the drawing.

4 Next, draw the roof of the car by rounding off the top and sides of the top box. Draw curved rectangles to make the windows.

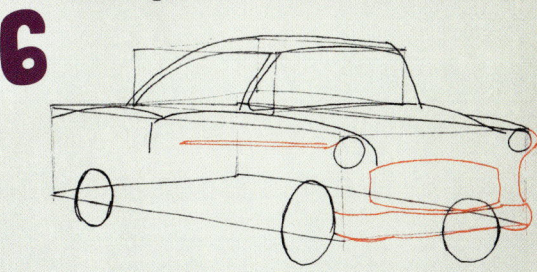

5 Now add curved lines to the top of the bottom box to shape the body of the Bel Air. Now draw two circles to the far right side, or front, of the bottom box to make the headlights.

6 Next, draw a line on the side of the lower 3-D rectangle. Draw a rectangle with curved sides on the front of the car.

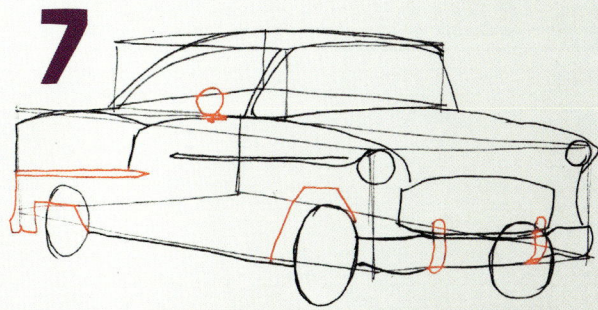

7 Draw the rearview mirror by making a small circle on the top side of the bottom box, near the middle to make the top of the car door. Draw a thin V-shaped line starting at the back of the bottom box and ending in the middle. Add two small curved rectangles to finish the bumper at the front side of the bottom box.

8 Add two vertical lines to make the windows. Draw a curved line at the top of the front side of the bottom box to make the hood. Add smaller circles inside the circles of the tires and headlights. Use horizontal and vertical lines to make the grille.

DRAWING THE SHELBY AC COBRA

In 1961, Carroll Shelby made the fastest sports car at the time, the Shelby AC Cobra. Shelby had gained a lot of experience and knowledge about cars from racing them. He dreamed of making a car that had the body of a British AC Bristol sports car with an American Ford V8 engine.

The result was the Shelby AC Cobra, which was introduced in 1962. The combination of the car's lightweight body and powerful engine helped it become a popular racing car. Soon after the success of the Shelby AC Cobra, the Ford company hired Shelby to make a special **edition** of the very popular Ford Mustang. This car became known as the Shelby GT-350 Mustang.

Early versions of the Shelby AC Cobra were clocked going from zero to 60 miles (96.5 km) per hour in about four seconds.

1 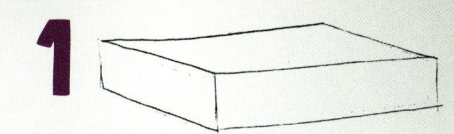
Start by drawing a long, flat box.

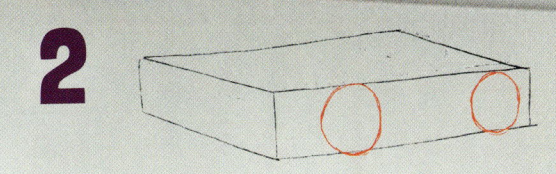

2
Now draw two circles on one side of the box to make the wheels.

3 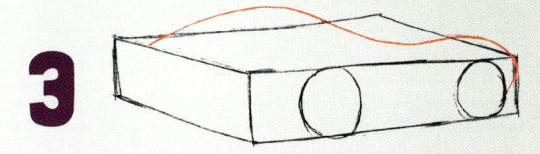
Draw a long wavy line across the rectangle to make the body of the Shelby.

4 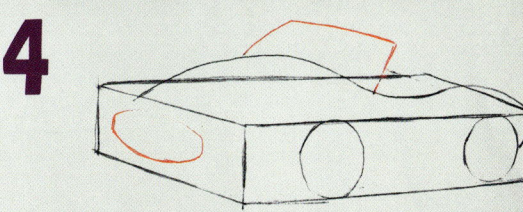
Next, draw three sides of a rectangle on top of the curved line to form the windshield. Draw an oval on the smallest side of the box to make the grille. This is the front of the Shelby AC Cobra.

5 
Draw two small circles near the oval for headlights. Draw curved lines out from the headlights toward the back of the car.

6 
Draw a curved line beginning under the grille and ending behind the back wheel. Then, draw a curved line behind the windshield.

7 
Draw circles within the circles to make the tires. Draw a small curved line to make the steering wheel. Now draw the **exhaust pipe** on the side.

8 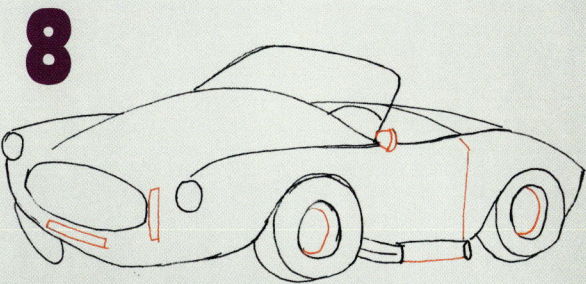
Add the rear view mirror next to the steering wheel. Next, add a curved line in the wheels to give them some depth. Add a small thin rectangle underneath the grille. Clean up any extra lines and you're done!

17

DRAWING THE MCLAREN F1

The idea for the McLaren F1 was thought up by race car designer Gordon Murray. The final car design, however, was done by Peter Stevens. The average top running speed of the McLaren F1 is about 237 miles (381 km) per hour! That's double the speed of most cars. In addition to being fast, the McLaren is expensive, too. It costs over $1 million! That's probably why only 106 McLarens were ever built.

The McLaren is not popular as a car for everyday driving because many features have been taken out so the car can go fast. The McLaren is a great race car, though. In 1995, a McLaren F1 won the famous Le Mans 24-hour car race.

The McLaren F1 is known as one of the fastest cars in the world!

1

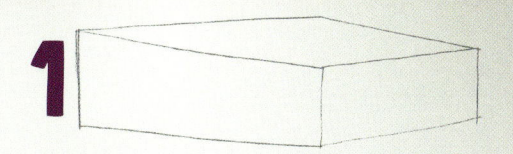

Begin by drawing a 3-D rectangle. Make the back slightly higher than the front.

2

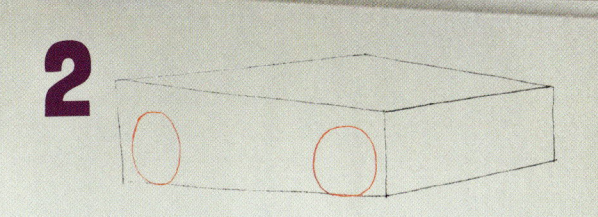

Now draw two circles for the tires.

3

Draw the roof by making the shape shown on top of the rectangle. Next, draw two lines in this shape to begin forming the windows.

4

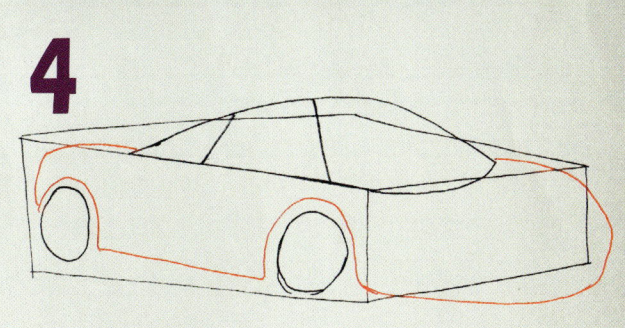

Draw the body of the McLaren by making a curved line circling the car.

5

Draw the windows by making the shapes shown. Draw two curved lines to make the steering wheel and dashboard.

6

Now draw the headlights as shown. Draw the bumper using curved horizontal lines.

7

Draw the design on the hood of the McLaren. To make the tires, add circles around the circles you drew for wheels.

8

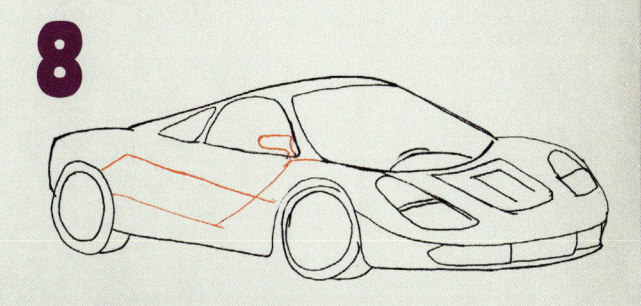

Add the rearview mirror. Draw the design lines on the side of the car. Erase any extra lines.

DRAWING THE PLYMOUTH PROWLER

In 1928, the Chrysler Motor Company introduced the first Plymouth car, with Amelia Earhart as its spokesperson. The Plymouth was named after the colony in Massachusetts set up by the Puritans, who sailed from England on the Mayflower in the 1600s. The word "Plymouth" represents the qualities of the Puritans—strength, honesty, determination, and achievement.

The Plymouth Prowler was a sports car first shown to the public at the North American International Auto Show in Detroit in 1993. The design is similar to the late 1930s classic American hot rods. By 1997 it was available to the public. The body of the Prowler was made entirely of aluminum, which was very advanced for that time. Chrysler stopped making these cars in 2002.

The aluminum body of the Plymouth Prowler was new and exciting, but the design was retro, which means copying the recent past.

1 Start by drawing a triangular shaped box.

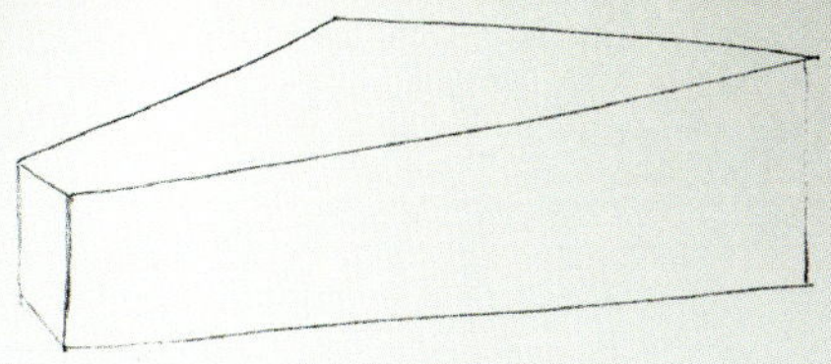

2 Next, draw three circles within the box. Notice their shapes, sizes, and where they are placed in the drawing.

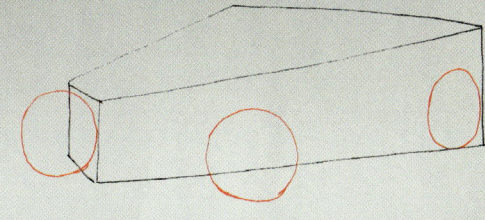

3 Now, draw a curved shape inside the triangular shape to make the body of the Prowler.

4 Draw a slanted rectangle for the windshield. Draw a curved line beginning from the back of the Prowler and ending at the tire.

5 Next draw two rectangles in the front to make the bumper. Draw a curved line at the tip of the Prowler to make the grille.

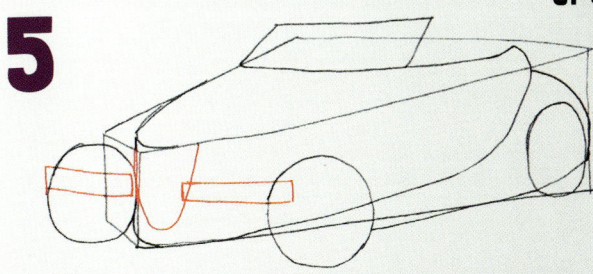

6 Now draw circles within the circles of the tires. Draw the fenders on top of the wheels. Draw a curved line from the grille.

7 Add a curved line for the steering wheel. Draw the rear view mirrors at either side. Draw two lines for the doors. Finally add lines going across the grille.

8 Erase any extra lines.

DRAWING TERMS

There are some words and shapes you will need to know to draw cars.

3-D box

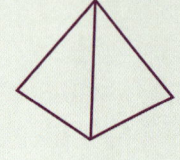

3-D triangle

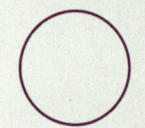

circle

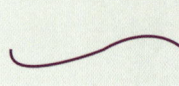

curved line

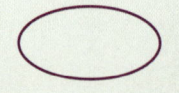

oval

rectangle

rounded rectangle

slanted line

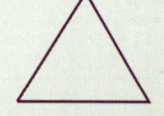

triangle

wavy line

GLOSSARY

assembly line: An arrangement of machines, equipment, and workers in which work passes down the line until the product is assembled.

differential gear: An arrangement of gears in automobiles that allows the two wheels on a single axle to turn at different speeds. This helps when turning.

edition: One of the forms in which something is presented.

engineer: Someone who plans and builds machines.

exhaust pipe: A pipe on vehicles that releases exhaust, or waste gases created by the engine.

hot rod: An automobile rebuilt or modified for high speed and fast acceleration.

ignition: A device used to start a car.

license plate: A metal plate on cars that shows it is legal to drive.

pace car: An automobile that leads the field of competitors through a pace lap but does not participate in the race.

V8 engine: A car's motor that has 8 slanted pistons positioned in two rows, forming a V shape.

INDEX

A
AC Cobra, 16, 17

B
Bel Air Sport Coupe, 14, 15
Benz Three-Wheeler, 4, 6, 7
Bugatti 41 Royale, 10, 11
Bugatti, Ettore, 10

C
Chevrolet, Louis, 14

D
Durant, William C., 14

F
Ford, Henry, 8
Ford Model T, 8, 9

M
McLaren F1, 18, 19
Murray, Gordon, 18

P
Porsche, Ferdinand, 12
Plymouth Prowler, 20, 21

R
Rolls-Royce, 10

S
Shelby, Carroll, 16
Stevens, Peter, 18

V
Volkswagen Beetle, 12, 13

WEBSITES

Due to the changing nature of Internet links, PowerKids Press has developed an online list of websites related to the subject of this book. This site is updated regularly. Please use this link to access the list: www.powerkidslinks.com/ltd/cars